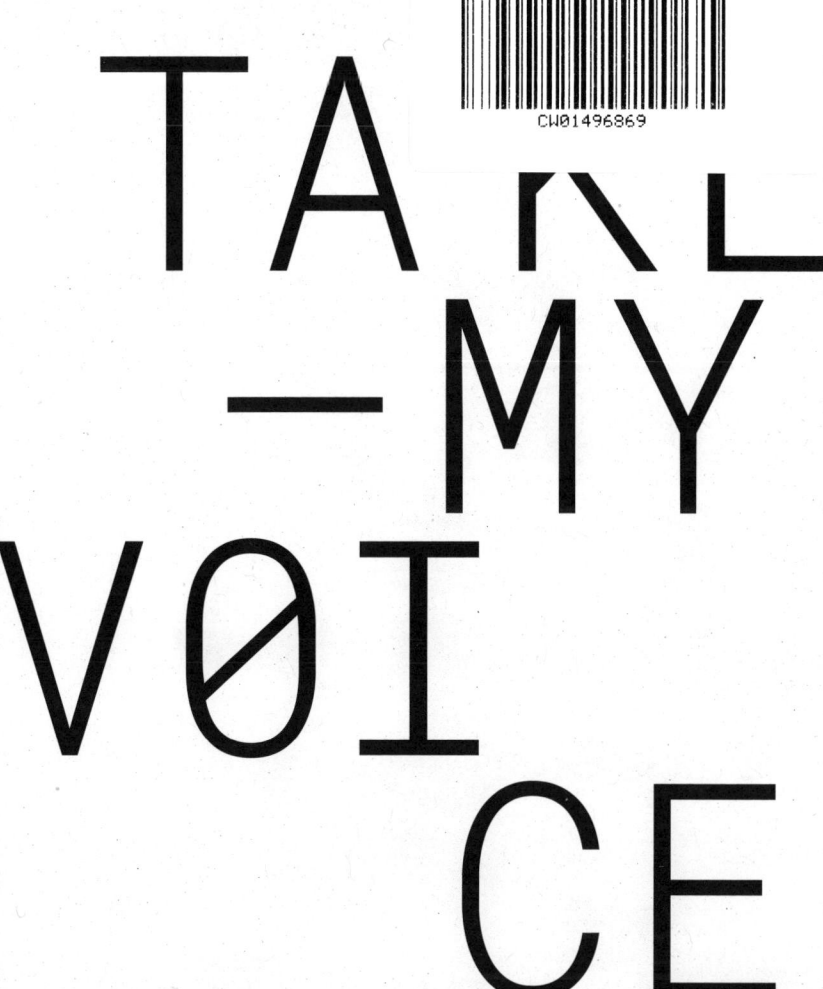

목소리를
드릴게요

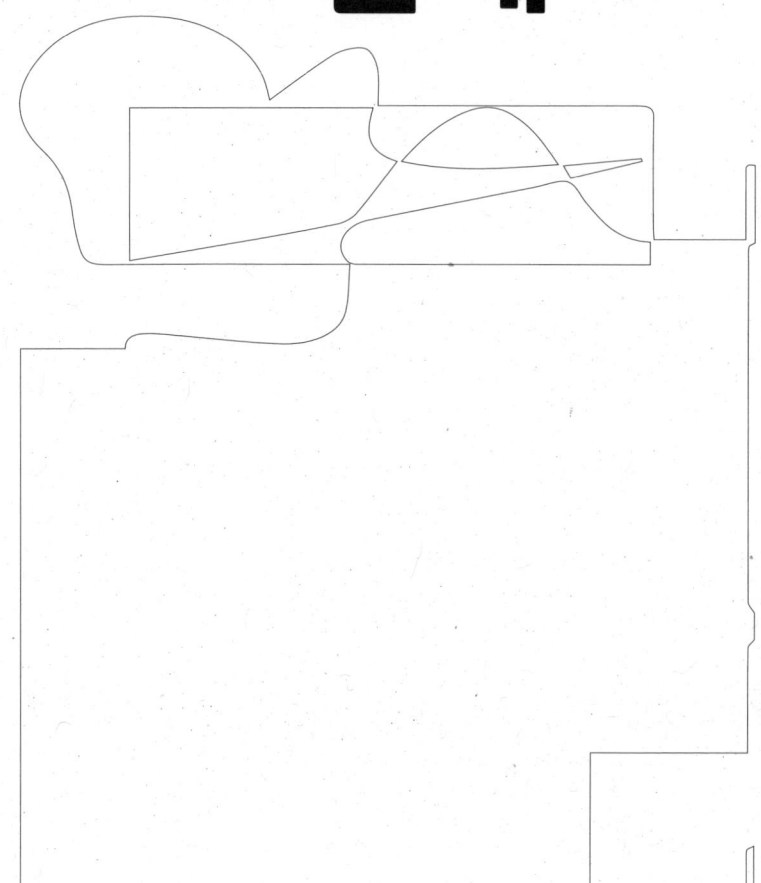

SERANG CHUNG
Translated by Anton Hur

Yeo Seunggyun (34, English teacher) couldn't remember his first day at the detention centre. He was highly sensitive to anaesthetics, but the government didn't make accommodations for such things. Seunggyun consequently lost consciousness for more than double the time of the average person on the same dosage.

Only on the second day of his internment could he manage the stiffness of his neck well enough to sit down at the warden's office.

"I believe, Teacher Yeo, that you understand our position."

The warden was a short man in his fifties whose easy smile reached his eyes. As small and neat as he was, there was a certain intimidating air about him—something like a little pocketknife, thought Seunggyun, still groggy and hungover from the anaesthesia.

"I'm, ah, actually not sure why I needed to be locked up?"

Well, he did have a vague suspicion, but to confirm it would mean he was in even more danger, so he tried hard to ignore his own thoughts.

"Teacher Yeo. Do you deny many of your students, sixteen to be exact, have become murderers?"

The warden's gaze was now sharp. Seunggyun squirmed in the uncomfortable chair.

This was, more or less, what he had suspected. News from students he had taught, for two years a contract teacher and four a permanent, was always disturbing. He hadn't known how many but some of the stories had made it to him. The first had been an "incident" during mandatory military service.

"But he was a gentle and quiet child," Seunggyun had said, "why would he have done this?"

"You know how it is," said the messenger, "still waters run deep. He actually shot his superior."

"But he didn't have a shred of violence in him."

People liked to say the military was better than it used to be. It could still be an awful place. And people can change. He didn't dwell on it. It was a broken world and there was little more one teacher could do except nurture good citizens and hope for the best.

Then there was one who pushed one of his college cohort down a rocky valley, and one who stabbed someone with a smashed beer bottle in a bar fight, and one who committed a hit-and-run under the influence, and one who strangled his victim during sex, and the suicide club organizer who gathered members into a room and left after everyone else had killed themselves, and one who had trapped and tortured someone in a subway bathroom stall, and the kidnapper-murderer, and the arsonist-murderer, and the one who installed a bomb in a subway station's coin locker, and one who mixed poison into IV bags and devastated an entire hospital, and one who'd worked on a construction site and dropped a large electric drill on a pedestrian, and one who worked at a grill and got into a fight with a customer before stabbing him with the tongs used to carry hot coal.

As much as they terrified him, they were at least out of sight; then his current students began giving him trouble. Two had got into a fight in which one died. Never before in the history of the school had this happened. It had even occurred during class. The boys had stabbed each other with shivs fashioned from pens and broken cleaning implements. The bloodstains on the linoleum were impossible to remove completely. Witnesses were in therapy for a long time. Not to mention the helpless teacher who had been permanently censured.

Seunggyun moved to an all-girls' high school on a hunch. One that was giving him an ulcer. A premonition that something was very, very wrong with him and made him sleepless and nauseous during the early hours. His world was being made an absolute hell as an example. To show how horrible people could be. He wasn't a passionate educator, but he did feel for his students. So he moved to a girls' school thinking the incidents might stop. It was a mistake. Girls could be murderers too.

"I know it's statistically… odd." Said Seunggyun, "but it's not like I did anything to make it happen. And they weren't all in my VLE."

This feeble objection brought the smile back to the warden's eyes. "It's actually your voice."

"My voice?"

"Whether they were online students or not, they had all heard your voice for more than six months."

"But I can't have been their only teacher?"

"Our agents have been watching you for a long time. We did an experiment at a forensics lab with a voice sample. To children with latent violent tendency, your voice was shown to have a kind of stimulating effect. It's not some unique frequency or anything, but there's just something about your voice that awakens the murderer within. Not your face, or smell Your voice."

They had collected his smell, too?

"But… even if true, it wasn't my intention. I have committed no crime myself? We live in a democracy! Where is this place even, where am I?"

"We can't tell you. But we have no intention of keeping you

목소리를 드릴게요

here indefinitely. All we need is your voice."

"What?"

"You must agree to having your voice box removed."

Seunggyun lost his voice anyway for a moment. Even if is was a reasonable compromise, and all this were true, it was still a shock.

"But," he sputtered, "I'm a teacher. If that happens—"

"We'll pay you a pension. And find you another job. One where you don't need to use your voice. You don't have to decide now. Take a few days."

"What happens if I refuse?"

"You're currently said to be in long-term, on-site training. Should you refuse the surgery, your family will receive a notification that you died in a car accident abroad and you will remain here indefinitely. We'll try to make things as comfortable as possible for you, but please, do give it some thought."

O

Seunggyun couldn't work out where the detention centre was located. Its walls weren't that high but he couldn't see a thing on the other side. Not even the tops of trees—just a sky the colour of rotten milk. No topographical cues. There was no smell of saltwater, which meant he wasn't on an island. The detention centre also had no peculiar characteristics, it was just a generic medical institution. It was also so small that no one would think much of it from the outside. Just some cheaply built corporate training centre.

The food wasn't as bad as he expected. He had imagined subsisting on cabbage and fish soup, like Ivan Denisovitch, but it wasn't like that at all. Despite the changing century, there must still be places like that in the world. But South Korea had moved on, at least, he marvelled. The quality was even higher than the also much-improved school lunches. Fish-cake soup one day did not mean spiced-up fish-cake soup the next; a varied and balanced meal appeared every time. Perhaps the lack of inmates allowed for higher-quality and more types of ingredients and generous portions. What a great country, he would mumble every time he sat down to eat. Of course, the fact he was peripherally responsible for sixteen murderers and thirty or more victims should probably have condemned him to death, so that he had a choice at all was something to be grateful for.

It was peaceful and quiet. There was no forced labour and each inmate had their own space and preoccupations, which meant they rarely ran into each other. Which was why the other inmates took a little getting used to.

The first was a 'hair mobilizer' named Jung Hamin (21, from Daejeon, unemployed). He seemed friendly.

"Ah, the warden kept saying Teacher Yeo, Teacher Yeo, but it's not yeo as in woman, it's your family name, Yeo—you're a man! How disappointing. So, how do you find yourself here?"

Seunggyun explained, in the vaguest language possible.

"So for you it's your voice box. It's hair, for me. I have to agree to getting all of my hair lasered off if I want to leave."

Hamin had been preparing for his university entrance exams near Daejeon. This was his second time trying, but he didn't give an impression of diligence. What he was really into was astronomy and he had even managed to procure a small telescope of his own.

"I lived in a commercial district. I couldn't see the stars or anything. It's the light pollution. There was a spot in the middle of a rice field I would go to, but then—they built streetlamps there! I was shocked. I get that it's a safety thing, but was it necessary to install so many?"

목소리를 드릴게요

For a month Hamin thought how great it would be if those damn streetlamps would just disappear. He stomped and shed hair while thinking such thoughts all over the street and soon the people walking those same streets would find themselves having those same bad thoughts about streetlamps, which then lead to violent behaviour. Some threw stones, others cut power lines, and one person even ran into one with a truck. Every streetlamp within a five-kilometre radius was damaged. Even some traffic lights.

"I'm glad it was just streetlamps. Can you imagine if I'd hoped if all the dogs and cats had disappeared? Or old people, or foreigners, or some other group of people? Can you imagine how awful that would've been?"

Despite his dark powers, Hamin seemed thankfully to have good morals; he looked genuinely terrified by what could've happened.

"You must've had other thoughts before? Had you no idea you had this ability?" Seunggyun himself hadn't known the extent of his own powers until more recently, it's true, but Hamin's ignorance still struck him as odd.

"Oh, I guess they didn't tell you? Our abilities generally develop after our nineteenth birthday. Isn't that strange? Which must be why they had adulthood rites at that age. Our ancestors must've known a thing or two"

"But hair. Can't you just wear a wig or something? Some people get their eyebrows tattooed on."

"What are you talking about? Hair is really important."

"More so than freedom?"

Seunggyun was asking Hamin questions he should have been directing to himself.

"They say if I get my laser treatment they'll exempt me from military service and give me a degree from a national university. So I guess I'll get treated eventually. I just want to take a break for a bit. I told my parents I was going on a foreign exchange programme as soon as I got into uni. As if such a thing existed in the world! Good thing they're not into details."

"No one suspects?"

"The agents here photoshopped some really great images to make me look like I was overseas."

Hamin's relaxed attitude was infectious. Seunggyun realised how nice it might to be to lay low for a while.

o

The second inmate he met was the elder of the place, super-spreader Kim Kyoungmo (64, from Pohang, entrepreneur).

"Oh look, a young person!"

Having heard about him previously, Seunggyun was reluctant at first but gripped and shook the hand proffered.

Kyoungmo spread viruses and germs of all kinds while never getting sick himself. People would die of the most fatal symptoms. Thinking the deaths around him meant he was just very unlucky, or indeed lucky, Kyoungmo eventually called the authorities himself when the death toll had reached truly ludicrous numbers. At the time, there was no system in place so authorities created the current one with input from Kyoungmo and others who had turned themselves in. In a sense, Seunggyun and the other detainees were now living in a system Kyoungmo had devised. So Kyoungmo had a different air—one of a person who had walked into the detention centre of his own accord, having lost everyone dear to him. Whether still or moving, he seemed to exist in a bubble of heavy air.

"I don't transmit anything to fellow monsters," he added reassuringly. The word "monsters" made Seunggyun flinch.

"Furthermore," said Kyoungmo, "there's no in-depth research

but there was one who died of lung cancer. Look, I'm smoking like a chimney myself, but I'm clean."

Before he entered the centre, Kyoungmo had run a billiards room that was always filled with smoke. He passed on his lit cigarette to Hamin, who passed it on to Seunggyun. Thinking it was some kind of initiation, Seunggyun took a few polite drags. He hoped it wasn't obvious he was a non-smoker. Kyoungmo watched him wordlessly and went back to his room alone.

"I don't understand," said Seunggyun to Hamin. "If he's a super-spreader, how come the warden or the other maintenance staff don't get infected? They also don't seem to be affected by you or me."

Hamin had been institutionalized only a few months before, but he spoke with the light confidence of an old hand. "They're cyclopses."

"Uh… I think they all have two eyes… ?"

"No, I mean figuratively, they only see one thing, tunnel vision. They don't have any special powers but, if you give them one specific focus, they will do anything. A different kind of monster from us, but still monsters. We have a kind of collective immunity."

The one specific focus wasn't, as Seunggyun first suspected, the usual fetishes of money, power, or honour. Hamin explained that, from what he'd seen so far, these fetishes tended to be things like rare model submarines, endangered plants, 17th century antique vanity cases, crystals that were useless but complicated to obtain, things that seemed rather arbitrary.

"But that's the low-level guards. No one knows what the warden 'cyclopses' over. It's a big secret around here. That Mr. Kyoungmo might know something."

Seunggyun was intrigued. He'd always needed more focus in his life. But imagining himself as proactive and productive was beyond him.

"The cyclopses are identified early and put to work in shady institutions like this one. They're civil servants, basically. If they happen to have an obscure fetish, the government indulges it so they can work. It's a really efficient system if you think about it. They've never so much as spread a single rumour about this place or our existence."

"But isn't it sad to have just one such focus your entire life?"

"Apparently not. They told me all sorts of saints and greats were cyclopses. I think they have a pride in what they do."

This reminded him of his girlfriend. Why don't you have any pride in what you do? she had once asked him in a chilly voice. They'd been in a fight when he was kidnapped. He had no idea what they could be said to be in now.

O

The hardest inmate to befriend had been the young ghoul.

"So what's your power?"

"I'm a ghoul."

"You're a girl? I can see that."

"No, the thing that eats dead flesh. Ghoul."

Before he'd been introduced, Seunggyun had seen the child with long hair from afar several times. Usually she carried a small spade and did some gardening. It had been unimaginable to him that she'd be one of them and Seunggyun had simply wondered what a child would be doing in the institution. He had never bumped into her in the cafeteria and had assumed the little girl to be a child of one of the workers. When he understood the ghoul's meal habits everything made sense.

Lee Suhyun (11, from Wonju, uncategorized) would not look Seunggyun in the eye. It was unclear whether this was

14   characteristic of Suhyun herself or generally characteristic of a
ghoul. She looked young for her age. It was said she wouldn't grow
much bigger than her current form.

"We do a lot of burrowing. Getting bigger isn't useful for that."

She looked a little damp, her hair was perpetually in tangles,
she had rows of sharp teeth and her back was bowed. From
afar, she looked like an ordinary child but, up close, there was no
denying what she was. The teeth were numerous, at least eighty.

First contact between humans and ghouls was in the middle
east. They'd spread through trade networks all over the world,
including the Korean peninsula where they'd settled during the late
Unified Silla and the early Goryo dynasty. They'd survived through
to Suhyun's parents' generation at which point they'd discovered
that obtaining a citizen registration number increased their
likelihood of not being killed. Ghoul babies looked human enough,
as their teeth hadn't come in yet, so they could easily be
registered as citizens and this had lowered the numbers of ghouls
massacred on sight.

"We don't kill people! What's wrong with eating humans if
they are already dead? What's the difference between that and
bacteria eating a corpse?? In fact I'm probably less dangerous than
bacteria!"

Suhyun didn't seem to enjoy life in the institution. But she
said that the funereal trend towards cremations rather than
interment had left graveyards full of soot and bones, so she was
staying put for now. There was some confusion as to whether
she was being held or protected. The government did a great job,
as usual, of taking care of its citizens by providing Suhyun with
corpses donated to science. Suhyun would bury the body parts
in the garden to let them age, and at one point had launched into
a detailed spiel about different parts needing different aging
periods which Seunggyun felt was unnecessary to know and

made him queasy.

Aside from these uneasy thoughts, however, Seunggyun felt sorry for her. The girl didn't seem to sleep, spending her days and nights turning over the dirt at the edge of the institution grounds. Since ghouls traditionally dined at night, she ate alone—although she'd probably have to anyway. But it was sad for any young girl to have to prepare her own meals and have no friends her own age to play with.

O

Seunggyun hadn't planned to stay for long. The prospect of surgery was worrying but it wasn't like he had a real choice in the matter and in truth he was resigned to undergoing the operation. All he wanted was a little more time before it happened, and wasn't he owed at least a holiday considering his imminent sacrifice for the greater good?

He was paid his regular salary and the environment was spacious and clean. But it had been hard weaning himself off the internet and his hands had shaken from withdrawal for the first few days. All of his email and messenger replies were dictated for the guards to send for him. Not that anyone tried to contact him much. Webtoons, webnovels, and webdramas had to be scrolled for, clicked, and watched with a guard. They weren't censoring his consumption but were concerned he would try to contact someone on the outside. Seunggyun worried the cyclops sitting with him might be bored to death or quietly mocking his taste, but it was better than nothing. Shopping was the same. A screen would be projected onto the wall and he would tell the guard where to click. He had never been much of a shopper but for some reason made an impulse purchase of a karaoke machine. When the guard hovered the cursor over a small blue microphone-style machine,

he demanded, "No, not that one, the big one, the proper one."
It took four days to ship.

He was hardly a decent singer but enjoyed going to noraebangs and was often told how good he was at creating a festive atmosphere. He was ready to learn sign language and carry around a writing pad for the rest of his life but for now he wanted to sing as much as he could before the inevitable. Like the teacher he had been, with his extremely thorough lesson plans, he decided to start from the beginning of the song-list and make his way through a page of the catalogue a day, singing only the songs he was familiar with. Usually there were about five a day, occasionally none, or other times twenty. He sang alone in his room so as not to disturb anyone but Hamin often dropped by, as well as occasionally Kyoungmo to sing a couple of songs themselves. In this way, along with all the TV they were allowed to watch, he became familiar with more of the latest hits, and so the centre kept ordering add-on pages for the catalogue, which is how he ended up staying at the centre far longer than he'd expected.

After breaking up with his girlfriend, singing love songs became a little more difficult. He'd wanted to break up over the phone but the centre forbade him. He did it over a short text, which likely meant, among their friends, that he was notorious in the outside world by now. His hope she might forget him completely was sincere. His mind had cleared during his time in the centre. His girlfriend was just too good for him. Anyone could see that. The only reason Seunggyun had had a chance was because men were so underrepresented in primary school teaching. His girlfriend had been clever, emotionally mature. She grew up in a nurturing household where for example they would put on an English conversation programme on the telly each morning and all watch it together. Whereas Seunggyun had long ceased contact with his scattered relations, watched trash television deep into the night, and felt so depressed some mornings that he would often call in sick. They both looked like responsible people from the outside but Seunggyun's diligence was mainly due to a desperate effort to overcome his environment and character whereas, for his girlfriend, it came more naturally. The longer they went out, the more his girlfriend must've realised it. What on Earth am I doing with this loser? Some languages are spoken without words. The language of regret, for example.

His heart was broken but if asked if he wanted things to go back to the way they were, to sacrifice his voice to see her again like he was a version of the Little Mermaid—the answer was no. Seunggyun shook it off and asked a guard to photoshop his images from "overseas" so they looked extra cool to aid her hate-scrolling.

It was around then when he first mumbled a new thought to himself out loud.

"Should I never leave?"

The voice was so low he almost thought it was someone else's. Or like his own subconscious was trying to talk to him.

"I mean. Should I just, never leave?"

This sentence kept coming from time to time in a low voice, and Seunggyun found his thoughts running in a new direction. His life was satisfactory at the centre. Dry, modest, never having to see anyone he didn't want to. The people he most wanted to avoid were his family. All they did was fight and hurt each other, ruining each other's mood. The problem stemmed from his rich landowner grandfather whom upon his death had bequeathed his legitimate children the most expensive territory while leaving Seunggyun's father, an illegitimate son, a sandy stretch of useless land. Soon after, it had leapt in valuation after a development project landed in that area. The jealousy among the offspring was such that it was a surprise they didn't resort to knife fights when the family gathered. His father, whose childhood had been marred by his illegitimacy, had ruined his own family as well. Seunggyun was, after all, an illegitimate child himself. His father had used the money from the developed land to set up a screen-golf range near Bundang where he seduced his mother, who had been a popular hagwon teacher. Seunggyun was born before his father's first marriage and his attempts to connect with his half-brother and half-sister were cruelly rejected. His mother did not take well to marriage and had divorced his father as soon as Seunggyun was in elementary school. Sorry that she had abandoned him, she always sent him expensive gadgets on his birthday but this wasn't enough for Seunggyun. Neglected by everyone, he grew up in the green screens of his father's golf range. His easy affinity for the centre was probably thanks to this upbringing, from the days of picking up broken golf balls and drinking canned sugary drinks for lunch. The thought of having disappeared overseas, or being presumed dead, was an intriguing prospect. He had acquaintances, but nothing he would call a deep friendship. Every night he thought back ten, twenty years trying to remember anyone he wanted to see again, but there was nobody. Not a single person for whom he would wish to lose his voice.

So wasn't he better off where he was? A detention centre, yes, but they even gave him two cans of beer every Saturday evening and left him alone to watch television late into the night if there was an away football game on.

So Seunggyun decided to stay put at the centre for now and ordered himself a mirrorball and some coloured spotlights.

О

The others also enjoyed their hobbies. Hamin, like many his age, owned every game console on the market. He was prevented from gaming online but was allowed to play anything otherwise available. Seunggyun didn't enjoy gaming himself and tired of it after a few hours. Not Hamin. He would appear at the cafeteria late into the afternoon, his eyes bloodshot. Seunggyun was fascinated by this contradiction with his normally easy-going demeanour: the boy had nowhere to go, couldn't he save his gameplay a little? Out of politeness Seunggyun would generally accept his invitations to join him, but that was all.

Kyoungmo, who had been here before even the warden, was basically best friends with the man. They played go, Chinese chess, Western chess, poker, go-stop, and all kinds of other board games. Seunggyun joined them a few times before being cowed by their years of expertise and high stakes. Money meant nothing inside the centre but Seunggyun hated to up the ante anyway. This was less about his relationship with money and more about his general timidness. Kyoungmo also had a fancy billiard set in his room that he had brought from his former place of business. He was practically a pro and Seunggyun, whose acquaintance with the sport had been only casual, was able to properly learn for the first time. The super-spreader was not as gregarious as the germs that seethed within him, but he was still a good teacher.

Suhyun collected zombie movies. When she wasn't tending to her corpse garden, she was rewatching one of these. The sight of a tiny ghoul watching films in a room that was darkened even during the daytime was exceedingly creepy. Suhyun seemed to regard the movies as appetizing food porn. Well-aged food walking around on screen, like home delivery on its own two feet. Seunggyun and Hamin would try watching with her in monsterly solidarity but Hamin's palpable terror at every close-up disturbed Seunggyun so much he couldn't continue. Not to mention Suhyun's hair always smelling of the earthy grave. In the end, Seunggyun expressed his solidarity and friendship by other means, buying Suhyun every new zombie movie he could as they were released. Suhyun would politely accept them and neatly floss her two rows of sharp teeth as she watched.

There was also plenty of television, radio, books, magazines, newspapers, or any other kind of 'old' media that only went 'one way'. Time stood still in the centre. Mealtimes were taken up with talk of what they had watched the day before and no one was interested in the news, though travel programmes were devoured. More than the people of the world, they missed its landscapes. And the popular music programmes—Seunggyun learned every note and line of every song, including rap, which made him wonder if he was a genius or just a bit sad. In the case of radio, they could make requests under supervision using messages fewer than three lines long. It reduced him to tears when the DJ played his song, but that was rare. And they had enough books to open a district-level library, and furthermore were regularly supplied with new releases and periodicals. The books were clean, there were no waiting lists, and no one bothered them about returns. They subscribed to so many papers and magazines it was almost surprising the outside world did not investigate where all those publications were going to.

It must've cost the taxpayer a pretty penny. Seunggyun, like any good civil servant working in education, felt a little guilty, but then changed his mind. They were paying society with their very freedom, he reasoned. Which it turns out was more valuable than he had realised. He decided not to deny himself his rightful compensation.

O

This peaceful state of affairs was interrupted by the arrival of another inmate.

Shin Yeonsun (27, from Namyangju, magazine intern) was accused of inducing addiction in the people around her. From alcohol, drugs, and caffeine to more complex addictions like gambling, sex, gaming, shopping, and, in one peculiar case, tuna, which ended in a man's death due to mercury poisoning. As a result of these various addictions, five were dead and over forty were being treated. Despite extensive research, the authorities couldn't determine the mechanism whereby Yeonsun distorted her victims' frontal or insular cortexes, it was just statistically likely based on models since devised that she had and did.

"Look, just tell me, explain it to me one more time. Give me the scientific evidence. Don't you have a report or something? Come on! I'm the victim here! Stop trying to fob me off... Look, all you have is a guess! How can you imprison someone because of a guess? The real person responsible might be walking around outside right now—Jesus! What the fuck! I thought things were looking up, now it's all ruined because of this stupid shit!"

For two weeks upon her arrival, Yeonsun cried and screamed the house down. Her reaction was, if anything, refreshing. Seunggyun and the others had been shocked by their imprisonment but they had considered their respective pasts and more or less accepted their fate, but not Yeonsun. No one had ever pounded the door or thrown a fit like she did. Even the cyclopses seemed mildly bothered as they sedated her, and the warden often came to her room to check up.

"A mistake, you say. Well, we've never had one of those before, but I suppose there's a first for everything. Let me convey your complaint to my superiors."

That was the best he could do. A few days later, the warden's unimaginable superiors sent word that they would assign a live-in research specialist. Yeonsun had to stay put until this researcher could determine beyond doubt that she was not a threat to society.

"What? After all the pointless poking and prodding, you're assigning one person to my case? Don't you realise how ridiculous you all sound? This is a violation of my human rights!"

Despite the screaming and the copious sobbing, Yeonsun showed up to the cafeteria, dragging her feet, a wan smile on her face. The rest of them could finally get a good look. She was the opposite of extraordinary, appearance-wise: perfectly ordinary features in a kind of strange balance such that, once they took their eyes off her, they couldn't remember what she looked like at all. None of them could be sure to recognize her on the street or whether her face was the same the next time they met. This inability to remember her face would leave an itch in their brains.

Hamin, who had given her a good look, leaned over toward Seunggyun and whispered, "It's obvious, no? It's her face! You keep having to look at it. That's what's conditioning the addictive behaviours."

"I dunno. Don't stare. She'll feel uncomfortable."

Seunggyun caught himself glancing at her from time to time. Yeonsun's appearance did appear to create a new tension in the room.

"By the way, hyoung, dating is strictly out of the question. Not just sex, but any kind of romantic... They keep mentioning the need to avoid unpredictable situations."

"Then shouldn't they separate us according to dating preferences?"

"How?"

"Well, maybe in combinations where our age differences would make dating out of the question, or... " His voice trailed off. Nothing else really came to mind.

"Apparently, we're not incarcerated at random anyway. They

try not to lock up people with overlapping abilities. I think they're worried about our powers causing feedback, or something."

"It must be tricky for the administrators."

How many more centres were there? How many of the inmates induced murder, like Seunggyun? He stared at the sky over the wall, wondering.

O

Yeonsun seemed to adjust to life at the centre. Not that she was any less determined to get to the bottom of the misunderstanding and leave, but at least she didn't try to make life difficult for the others. Which actually ended up in some amusing scenes.

Perhaps having judged Suhyun an easy first target, her being the youngest, Yeonsun was observed walking towards the corpse garden at a leisurely pace she had never exhibited before. Suhyun, thinking she was just passing through, ignored her.

But Yeonsun sat down on the bench right next to her and—without any greeting or preamble—grabbed her hair.

Everyone watching took a sharp intake of breath. Suhyun, obviously, was the most surprised. She made a strange sound like a field animal caught in the grips of a predator. Usually so reluctant to look anyone in the eye, she turned her gaze toward Yeonsun.

Untroubled by it all, Yeonsun started to braid the clump of Suhyun's hair. Realising Yeonsun's gesture was friendly and that she meant no harm, Suhyun sat still, if a little stiffly. She looked like she was biting down on her own tongue. Completely unaware of Suhyun's nervousness, Yeonsun continued to gently braid and disentangle her hair.

"Maybe we'll try a French braid instead?"

Suhyun made a kind of short growl that Yeonsun took as a

24 yes. As she carefully undid her hair and started over, silence fell
on the centre grounds and everyone pretended to go back to what
they were doing.

This then became a regular ritual at the centre. Whenever she
felt a food coma coming on and the sunlight came down hot in
the garden, Suhyun would relax in the cool basement level while
Yeonsun braided her hair.

o

She's not going to start braiding ours too, is she?
Needless to say, Yeonsun did not. But her next mission did
still have something to do with it. One day, Yeonsun went up to
Kyoungmo and gave him some beauty advice in a cheerful but firm
voice.

"I think if you let your five-o'clock shadow grow, you'd look a
bit like Mads Mikkelsen."

Not knowing who Mads Mikkelsen was, Kyoungmo picked up
his coffee mug and fled to his room. Yeonsun was not the type to
give up easily. She mentioned it every time she bumped into him,
recruiting everyone around her in her efforts.

"Mr. Hamin, you think he'll look better that way, right? And you,
Teacher Yeo, don't you agree?"

A guard googled Mads Mikkelsen's name and showed
Kyoungmo an image result. Kyoungmo initially grimaced, but
acquiesced and started to let his beard grow. There were a few
patches of white, but the overall effect did indeed suit him rather
well. He looked more like a respected proprietor of a fashionable
café than that of a billiards hall.

Yeonsun's next conquest was Hamin, against whom she
won almost every videogame. She broke through effortlessly into
higher levels, found all sorts of hidden cheats, loaded herself with

coins and items, and felled every boss. Her reflexes surpassed the imagination and her luck was timely. Hamin's pride fell through his stomach, but, being young as he was, it took only a few hours to recover. Having a competitor ultimately brought new life to his gameplay.

"Rematch! Seunggyun hyoung ruined my touch!"

Yeonsun seemed a little shyer around Seunggyun at first, as he wasn't as approachable as Hamin. But she soon found a way in. He was unable to continue his karaoke project as Yeonsun took over the machine, declaring there to be nothing like singing to aid the digestion. For some reason she kept singing trot music; she had a tolerable voice but it wasn't quite right for the genre. The reason Seunggyun never suggested she just get a machine of her own was because of the conversations they sometimes had between songs.

"I had a dream last night. My head was on my mother's lap and I was drifting off to sleep. Weird, right? That I'm in a dream and I'm still sleepy? My mother kept saying, Don't go to sleep, don't go to sleep. I kept wondering why when I began to think that what she really meant was, Don't wake up, don't wake up. Because we wouldn't be together anymore if I woke up."

Yeonsun had lived with her mother before coming to the centre, just the two of them. Having worked for years at a company that made small electronic parts, her mother had scrimped and saved enough to raise her and support her through college. When Yeonsun said she'd get a part-time job, her mother insisted she study more instead and aim for a scholarship. Yeonsun ended up winning several. And when she couldn't afford school, she simply took a semester off. It had been devastating when she had managed to graduate but couldn't get a job for a long time. And just when she had scored an internship, she had been dragged in here.

"Teacher, did you know that companies are using interns for all sorts of horrible work? But mine offered proper training. I once had one of those zero hours municipal internship con-jobs, though. I was assigned to a zoo. I thought I'd be working on their ads or pamphlets or something that had to do with my actual studies. I mean, I believe zoos should be abolished, but I decided to persevere for the sake of supporting my mother, but they ended up putting me with the zookeepers! I had to get up at four in the morning to chop up the root vegetables for the bears and clean their cages, can you imagine?"

"Bears are cute."

"Yes, baby bears and even the grown-up bears, at least the smaller ones, are adorable. I got really attached to them, to be honest. They kind of cling to your knees and it's annoying when they tear your jeans but I could see why teddy bears were invented. But the big ones, they're scary. I saw a zoogoer almost lose an arm! I was in no position to be picky and I needed something, but what was working with the bears going to do for my résumé? I felt so sorry for the trapped bears and so sorry for myself trapped with them... Those government programmes, they're nearly all like that. I finally managed to find one that wasn't... they really liked me and were going to give me a permanent position... Teacher, I really was going to get settled down, give my mother a rest."

The agents had hurt Yeonsun's feelings saying her mother had been addicted to work, taking as much overtime as she could and a part-time job on top of her regular one. Yeonsun was unable to determine, or perhaps admit, that she had been the one to drive her mother to work-addiction, that it was her fault her mother's hands and feet were so swollen every morning.

"I'm sure you'll see her again someday," said Seunggyun, not knowing what else to say.

"To be honest, Teacher, I don't know if I'll ever make it out of here. If I could, I'd do anything, honest. At least it feels better talking to you about it."

Seunggyun felt uncomfortable with how deferential Yeonsun was being, calling him "Teacher" all the time. He wasn't a teacher anymore, after all, and, as they were both adults, the deference seemed unnecessary. But because the stories Yeonsun would tell him between the karaoke machine's fanfare and the intro to the next song were told only to him, he didn't say anything. Making the excuse that he didn't want to disturb the others with the singing, he had his room soundproofed so they could have more privacy in their chats. He wanted to keep their time just to themselves. He even found himself glad they were incarcerated. As long as he was with Yeonsun, he wasn't alone. Incarceration was, if anything, a kind of intimacy. He was at a loss whenever the other inmates butted into their time together.

Yeonsun made every day at the centre special. She proposed they each take turns cooking a dish for all the inmates every weekend, getting the warden's permission to do so. The guards were watchful that the inmates should not cause a riot with the cooking utensils, but nothing of the sort ever happened. And while the scheme had been Yeonsun's suggestion, the other inmates rose to the challenge gladly. Kyoungmo made North Korean-style dumplings in spiced soy sauce, Seunggyun made spicy sujaebi, Yeonsun mixed rice in oven-cooked sweet pumpkins, and Hamin made rabokki in jjajang sauce. Suhyun would take one bite of each and spit it into a napkin, but she enjoyed sitting with them. It was a fun activity for about a month, but, out of consideration for Suhyun who had to eat alone in the garden at night with the lights turned off, they eventually decided not to continue with it.

Next, Yeonsun arranged a sports day between all the inmates and the guards, which ended up becoming mostly a sports day for the guards, but a grand time was had by all. The warden had promised a bonus for any cyclops who did well, and that had had a profound effect. Unexpectedly, however, Suhyun beat all comers at arm-wrestling, which in retrospect shouldn't have been a surprise as she was digging all hours and dragging around corpses several times her size.

A barter system was established within the centre, old window blinds and lightbulbs were replaced with energy-efficient solutions, a rainwater recycling system installed, dance times instituted for every second and fourth Friday of the month, a cyclops who could offer music lessons sourced, an art room was built—Yeonsun proved absolutely tireless in her efforts. To think that such a fantastic worker was so routinely relegated to a lowly internship! Everyone agreed the world outside this place must be mad.

Thus Yeonsun settled into life at the centre. Both the inmates and guards cared for her, and it felt like the centre had somehow always been preparing for her arrival. Now that she was here, Yeonsun assumed the role as a kind of mascot for the place. A symbol of its spirit. A queen whose face they couldn't help but stare at and who reigned over a peaceful and prosperous realm, to the praise of all her subjects.

o

It was a short golden age. Only in retrospect, and regret, was the progression of events apparent. Seunggyun would feel guilty about it for a long time. Yeonsun had fallen ill. At first they thought it was a simple cold, but she couldn't stop coughing. A light cough at first, then at some point, a rattling one. The infirmary diagnosed her with consumption.

"She really isn't the type to complain, that one, I wish she had! Things must've been so stressful for the poor thing," said

Kyoungmo, fretting, as he paced the corridor in front of the infirmary. Suhyun visited her with a bouquet of flowers from her corpse garden. Despite her bedridden state, Yeonsun still managed to take out her lip balm and gently apply it to the young ghoul's chapped lips. The most unjudging of all saints, her hands cared for even the most neglected monster. Seunggyun felt like doing the three thousand bows if he thought it would help her recover.

When she did finally start to get better, she contracted a skin infection.

"Great," she joked with a grimace, "I came to the infirmary to get better, but then the lack of sunlight gave me another disease."

Her humour in this situation was in keeping with her character. Boils started up from her ankles to her upper body. She took antibiotics s both orally and topically, which soon created a side effect in her kidneys. Her skin kept getting worse. Next came hepatitis-A. Then malaria. Chicken pox. Japanese river fever. This was when they began to realize something was very wrong. Yeonsun laughed it off, but no one laughed with her. Every night, a little bit more of the centre seemed to crumble away.

O

Of course, the first person to realise it was Kyoungmo. He stayed in his room, the highest room in the building, and never let anyone in. He blocked the floor crack in the door with a wet towel. It was a wonder air circulated in there at all. He cleaned his own utensils and, after asking for a small washing machine, he started doing his own laundry. The warden tried to convince Kyoungmo her sickness wasn't his fault, but he wouldn't even let him in the door. Kyoungmo shouted through the door so loudly the panel vibrated.

"It's your fault! I gave her the diseases. There is no other explanation. I can't believe you let this happen. I didn't want to make anyone sick. That's all I ever wanted. It's why I brought myself here in the first place and stuffed myself into a hole, but this stupid government… If Yeonsun is sick, that's proof she's not one of us! She can't be a monster."

Listening on the staircase nearby, Seunggyun didn't flinch at the word "monster" like he used to. Monsters were clearly what they were. Not in any self-pejorative sense, but a scientific one, monsters who have proven their monstrosity through their immunity against each other. How could there have been such a glaring error in the system?

Kyoungmo's rant went on. It was epic. He mentioned his parents, siblings, and childhood friends all dying the year he turned twenty-one, and the wife who eventually perished as well.

"I know how pathetic I am. I've lost so many people in my life I thought I deserved to have at least one. I was a fool. We wed only two months after meeting each other, and within two weeks she was in the ground. It should've been me… But what was this stupid country doing about it? I'd barely finished middle school, but even I realised what was going on faster than any of you useless bastards. Too busy spying on civilians when I was the person you really should've been spying on. You left all the monsters well alone and instead grabbed university students off the streets and tortured them instead! And, when I turned myself in, the first thing you do is to try to make me into a weapon! I didn't care if it was the Cold War and if trains ran on time, the first person to say so, I would pluck their tongues out of their heads.I lived through all of it, the whole shitshow, and now this— get mea fucking lawyer. I'm going to sue! No, shut up, I said I'm goingto sue!"

The warden tried to calm him down, saying he was talking with his superiors. But the inmates were sceptical as to whether a solution would arrive on time; Seunggyun and Hamin demanded

Yeonsun be transferred to another facility immediately, but they were told that this was impossible when they still didn't know exactly what was the nature of Yeonsun's monstrosity. Seunggyun wanted to punch the warden, or the walls, or throw things, but he did none of that. Hamin crept up towards him and sat down on a lower step.

"She has to be sent away," Seunggyun murmured.

"I agree. She might die if she stays. Who knows what even nastier diseases await, like advanced syphilis or the plague."

"But how? The cyclopses refuse to listen."

"If only we could get her out of here… I can take care of the rest."

"What? What do you mean?"

Hamin, apparently, was connected to some pretty powerful people. Somehow, during election season, a key player in the ruling party had caught wind of Hamin's power and came to visit. His mobilizing hair could be a secret weapon that could be used to affect the processes of democracy. It disturbed Hamin that such an interview had been set up at all, but he decided to make a deal so he'd have some cash on hand when he got out. And he was only breaking his confidentiality agreement now for the sake of helping Yeonsun.

"For a month I made myself think, 'Vote candidate 1' and 'Don't vote candidate 3', and gathered the hair that fell from my head for them to use in campaigning."

"That's awful."

"Some marketing strategists from a large conglomerate also visited recently—"

"You're lying!"

"No, really."

Such examples made Seunggyun wonder if the people outside would ever be able to find out what was wrong with Yeonsun.

"What if you have a stray thought?"

"Are you joking? This was business, I've never concentrated so hard in my life. I only did the shameful deed because the centre only matches your old salary on entry here and I needed cash for my future. But anyway. The point is, I wonder if I could still use those connections now? To help?"

"You think they'd help get Ms. Yeonsun out of here?"

"Yeah. I think it's the least they could do. Well, either that or assassinate me, but the first option seems more likely."

"I mean, assassinations are a little—"

"We can choose to believe Korea is a democracy. But we can also believe that democracy is a system, and all systems have people who could twist it or make or find a hole in it, if you know what I mean."

How could this clever young man not have made it into university? Seunggyun silently lamented this failure of the educational system.

O

Suhyun woke up Seunggyun in the middle of the night. Thankfully, he stopped himself screaming at the cold, damp, and twisted fingers shaking his shoulder, and the fact that she had caught him in his underwear. Seunggyun was always careful not to make his students uncomfortable or embarrassed.

"What happened?" whispered Seunggyun, pulling the sheets up to his neck. He considered asking the ghoul to respect his privacy but decided to leave it. "Has something happened to Ms. Yeonsun? How did you get up here without getting caught?" Whether it was from all the singing or the fact that his voice still hadn't recovered from the years of teaching, it still sounded grating even to his own ears.

"I walk around at night all the time, no one cares," Suhyun answered matter-of-factly. At night her eyes looked brighter and more alert. Perhaps she'd just had a good meal.

"I heard from Hamin oppa that you're trying to get Yeonsun unni out of here?"

"Yes. We just talked about it. No real plan exactly but if we don't, Ms. Yeonsun might—" die, he was about to say, but he wasn't sure how a ghoul might react to the prospect.

"Look, I like unni. I'm never going to eat her. I've never liked anyone so much I'd waste their meat like that."

"I see." He wondered how she felt about the rest of them.

"I have these underground tunnels."

"You have what?"

"Tunnels."

"To the outside?"

"Yes. To a cemetery nearby. Sometimes I like something that's aged particularly well. The bones have a nice crunch. Like slow-cooked ribs. So I dug a tunnel, just in case."

"So the centre doesn't know?"

"They don't. I block the entrance with bodies. No one digs that far down. No matter how thorough the guard. And they seem pretty preoccupied lately."

"Do you think Ms. Yeonsun might fit?"

"It's a bit small. But if you're serious I could work on it."

"But if you get caught… you could be in real danger."

She simply shook her head. Not to say she didn't think so, but rather that she was more than willing to pay that price. The braids that Yeonsun had made for Suhyun, even during her sickness, still hung around her face.

O

They needed a distraction. Kyoungmo decided to break his absolute quarantine rule and invited the warden into his room for poker. His strategy was to maintain the smallest difference in points and chips as he could to keep the warden engaged. While the cyclopses were strict, they were also not very proactive. Once the cyclops that handed down orders was preoccupied, the others would be more sluggish to respond.

"As long as I can keep contact with the outside world to a minimum, I will do whatever it takes," said Kyoungmo, his beard neatly trimmed despite self-isolation. This meant one fewer chess piece on the board but Seunggyun had to concede it was a good plan.

As the eyes watching Suhyun would be averted during dinner time, Suhyun would guide Yeonsun out of the tunnel while the remaining cyclopses were to be distracted by Seunggyun. Thankfully Yeonsun could still walk, and Suhyun, as demonstrated during the arm-wrestling contest, was more than strong enough to carry her should the need arise. Now all Seunggyun had to figure out was how to distract the guards.

"Can you get me some things I need?" Seunggyun asked Hamin after thinking it over for a few days. Because of the number of recent visits from outsiders, Hamin had taken to plucking his hair instead of waiting for hairs to fall out, leaving his hairline patchy. He looked down the list he was handed. A GPS device for driving, a portable speaker, underwater camera, an electric bicycle, and a radio-controlled dinosaur robot—nothing Hamin wouldn't ask to order on his own. Some of the items were obtained through the centre, some through gifts from the outside. He thought he might be able to smuggle a few more items through the latter method.

"Honestly, I stayed because I didn't want to be bald, and here I am nearly bald anyway. Who'd have dreamt things might turn out this way?" said Hamin with a sigh.

"Maybe we can pluck some of my hair instead for your clients?" suggested Seunggyun.

"You know I can't abide that sort of thing."

"You're a truly honest gentleman, Mr. Hamin. A rarity."

Despite his anxiety, each item passed through the centre censors without comment. They decided on a day and once the plan was finalised, they fully informed Yeonsun, with whom they now had to meet in hazmat suits because of her condition, which made conspiratorial whispers a little tricky.

"Thank you so much... all this trouble... I'll never find friends like you again."

The mumps disfiguring her face made her words difficult to say. With a rare moment of physical courage, he squeezed Yeonsun's hand through his hazmat suit glove. He looked into her eyes and hoped she could see their collective determination in his gaze.

As soon as they turned away, her face grew faint in his mind. But the sense of her hand in his own didn't grow faint at all. Not for a long time.

O

Even when Seunggyun had asked for a life jacket, none of the cyclopses had batted an eye. It would seem a reasonable suspicion when there was no swimming pool on the grounds, but they said nothing as they bought him a standard sized one for adults with four buckles.

Seunggyun and Hamin worked on the jacket in the art room quite brazenly, soldering on the various bits of equipment. The cyclopses continued to seem uninterested. Seunggyun had a cover story ready, but no one asked what they were doing. Handicrafts were, after all, encouraged by the authorities and they had been given nothing specific to look out for. And so the former English teacher and college entrance student managed to put together a pretty good rig. It was actually Hamin more than Seunggyun who was good with his hands. Seunggyun had had the idea, but Hamin had executed it very well.

"You have good hands."

"I think they're a bit of a waste in this centre, myself."

"I really would like to turn it on just once, to see if it works."

"Oh hyoung, you know very well we can't do that."

They didn't have to delay the day at all. On the promised night, Seunggyun put on the vest and stood in the middle of the centre's grounds. It was the farthest point from the corpse garden, and with the building between them. He looked up at the white building, its windows like black eyes opened to the night, and thought he hadn't really disliked his life here. Which made him realise all the more how completely his life was about to change.

"Testing, testing, one-two-three."

Next to the wall, in a shadow, Hamin nodded and gave a wave. He was wearing earphones, and the earphones were connected to a small radio.

And so began Seunggyun's illegal radio broadcast. At first, a little uncertainly.

"Hello… hello? Everyone? Whom do I mean by everyone… people of Korea, I guess? I'm, well, I can't really tell you who I am, and I don't really know where I am… I wish I did but I've no idea, and while I hope someone is listening, I also hope, almost as much, that no one is listening."

He was speaking on an obscure channel so it was doubtful many people would be listening at all, but still his voice was riding the waves, which wasn't allowed, however briefly. Seunggyun had remembered a small chapbook from college and had requested it, and the request had been granted. The chapbook, intended for activists, explained how to create a one-person radio station. A propaganda work inspired by America's radical media movement as portrayed in the film Pump Up the Volume, and the Telestreet movement in Bologna. Seunggyun had no idea if the independent publishers responsible were still around and printing these things, but he had been lucky and located a copy. Despite the advent of podcasts having supplanted the need, copies of the chapbook were still being circulated, just in case; thanks to this, he had managed to create a personal radio broadcast station that he could carry on a life vest. He had, effectively, weaponised himself. It was a threat. A threat against... what? The world?

So Seunggyun began his peripatetic pirate broadcast. His only hope was that, as the guards chased him, Yeonsun would be given time to escape. He had to keep talking and keep running convincingly enough for them to believe that Seunggyun, a person who had never given anyone trouble since his incarceration, was somehow newly set on doing extreme harm. His heart felt like it might pound right through his ribcage.

"I'm warning you though, my voice... Something about it lights, what's it called, a fuse? A fuse in your brain. I don't think it does that for everyone but it does it for a lot of people. You would have to listen to it for six months, I think, so I guess just one night shouldn't hurt? And who knows what effect it might have when distorted through a broadcast, but if you happen to feel particularly murderous tonight, please try to hold it in? Stay indoors alone? Don't hurt anyone? All right, what else can I talk about—"

Seunggyun was a good teacher, according to the evaluations of his peers and students. The information he needed to convey was set, and he was good with his lesson plans and well-practiced in delivering them. It was like singing, with its pre-arranged dynamics and melody. He had written a script the night before, but the inside of his brain had turned blank as a sheet—so he began to sing. Despite having practiced all the latest songs, he could only remember hits from the 90s and Noughties, English pop songs he taught in class. Lyrics engraved on his bones. He sang "Grab onto Her" despite this whole thing, and "Dream a Little Dream of Me" which he knew by heart even if he couldn't sing as well as a bird sitting in a sycamore tree. But it had been a great song for teaching English prepositions, and now the lyrics just flowed out of him.

As Seunggyun marched around in big strides and did stretches as he sang, the guards initially didn't show any dramatic reaction. This was expected; he wasn't shouting, and the microphone on his vest didn't look too obvious. The transmitter antennae stuck out from his back but it was black and apparently buried in shadow. The guards on duty seemed to be discussing things amongst themselves: Why was he wandering around in the middle of the night, singing? A couple of them walked unhurriedly toward the building. They were probably headed to talk to the warden, but the warden was in Kyoungmo's room. By now likely playing go-stop, the most fiercely immersive of the games. The guard would need at least five minutes in order to see that the warden's room was empty and then time to walk up to Kyoungmo's cell.

Around the time Seunggyun got to "As Much As the Love Sprinkled on This World," the order must've finally come down or perhaps the guards had caught wind on their own, as they suddenly charged him. Seunggyun ran, still singing. He zigzagged around the lawn, screaming out the words, but continued to stay as far away from the corpse garden as possible.

The guards managed to pounce on him by the time he was belting out "Chau Chau" by Deli Spice. It was eleven minutes into the radio broadcast. Leaping from the shadows, Hamin tried valiantly to take on a couple of the guards but without much success. At the very least, they had given them enough of a chase for the centre to regret ever providing treadmills. Overall, it was a better-than-expected result. Seunggyun was glad his face was being shoved into grass and not concrete but still had a nagging worry as to whether Yeonsun had escaped.

"Find the others!" shouted the warden, who suddenly looked like a giant standing in the front door. His eyes were so wide there was more whites than pupils, like he had revealed a hidden face—Seunggyun didn't care. He spat out dirt and gazed dispassionately at the broken components around him. If this didn't work, there would be other ways. They were going to get Yeonsun out of here, and he realised, for the first time, that true conviction brought one a peace close to numbness.

"And as for that bastard," the warden said, dropping honorifics for the first time, "that little fucking bastard—lock him up."

O

Seunggyun was locked in the basement. It was the first time he'd seen bars in the centre. He called out for Hamin, but there was no reply; he was probably put somewhere else. There was no clock but the appearance of three meals a day allowed him to discern the passage of time. The food was terrible. Surely it was made in the same kitchen by the same people, but it was bad enough to suspect it was deliberate. An implicit agreement had been broken, and actually Seunggyun didn't have a problem with that, having been the one to break it. The food must've been nutritious enough but his gums felt weaker. Perhaps because he hadn't seen the sun in a while, or maybe they'd been knocked loose when he'd been knocked down. It didn't matter either way. Everything else was fine. If only someone would tell him what had happened to Yeonsun. Seunggyun had to know if she had managed to crawl through the tunnel to safety. The guards were so strict. He wondered how much Hamin and Kyoungmo were also being punished, and whether Suhyun managed to come back all right. Surely children had to be treated like minors. If they discriminated against her for being a ghoul and were cruel to her, he swore to himself he would make them pay.

In between meals, during those times he started thinking of as night, Seunggyun's skin began to itch. Like tiny bugs crawling behind his ears, down his back, behind his thighs. He knew this was guilt. What if the radio broadcast had pressed someone's switch and turned them into a murderer?

But they had to have been exposed for at least six months to his voice, the authorities had said. Eleven minutes was just enough for a threat, but it couldn't have done any real harm to the population, but... wasn't there still the slightest chance... perhaps with someone particularly susceptible? Imagine if Seunggyun had happened to have been more broadcast-friendly previously, as a teacher, and had been selected for the Educational Broadcasting System? It didn't bear thinking about the potential consequences of such a thing. It made his hair stand on end. Seunggyun tried to scratch away his goosebumps.

When he was finally released, his face was so haggard he definitely would not have been considered broadcast-friendly.

"Wow, you look like a proper inmate now! The lights look switched off in your eyes," said Hamin as he handed him a basketful of gummi bears.

"What happened to Ms. Yeonsun?"

"Nuna managed to get out of here just fine. She was weak so it took a little longer than expected. By the time the people waiting at the cemetery picked her up, the guards were already all over the map. But they didn't know she was there, because they couldn't imagine there was a tunnel. Thank god it took her some time to get through it, if anything."

The warden had apparently conveyed the news to him, cracking walnuts in his bare hands. He had definitely not been in the mood for further questions.

"What about you, Mr. Hamin? Are you all right?"

"I was locked up on the fourth floor for a couple of days but then they let me out. Kyoungmo got a slap on the wrist and Suhyun is under 24-hour surveillance but she's not put away anywhere. They took away your karaoke machine, my games, Kyoungmo's billiards table, and Suhyun's DVD collection. Isn't that the worst?"

Hardly, Seunggyun wanted to say through his dry lips.

"I promised to help again during the byelections, which put a lot of pressure on the warden's superiors to let him off with a warning, and all's well that ends well, as they say. Hey hyoung, do you know what the warden's 'thing' turns out to be? I've only just learned it recently."

It was the fruit of a tree that grows in West Africa, only edible in oil extract form, and so bitter that only the warden wanted to eat it, with the tree itself near extinction. The trees brought into Korea needed a dedicated greenhouse and gardener, as well as a special extractor. The warden was not allowed in the greenhouse and could only receive the extract once a quarter, but the escape incident cut down his oil to half of what it used to be. And he had taken out his rage by confiscating the inmates' things. Probably the cruellest form of revenge to a cyclops, and it was the cruelty that had depressed Hamin, but Seunggyun was glad it wasn't worse. Because the one thing he couldn't abide was violence. But Yeonsun was safe. She wasn't going to be sick anymore. And he himself would walk around the outside world again, even if it meant never singing another note for the rest of his life. He walked around the centre and was happy to see that Yeonsun

목소리를 드릴게요

was not there. A real happiness, if a bit of a dull one. It took a bit of time for him to realise what that dullness meant.

For more than a month they had to eat the most terrible prison food, but eventually the warden got over it and things went almost back to normal. Cyclopses, as obsessive as they were, also seemed surprisingly good at letting go of things. The only real difference was that Kyoungmo gave up trimming his beard, letting it grow long and white like a wise man of the mountain. And Suhyun eventually mastered the art of braiding her own hair and now sported intricate patterns that crisscrossed her scalp. It was the monsters' way of reminding themselves of her.

O

"I'm ready for the surgery now."

The warden seemed to have expected this from the moment Seunggyun had requested an interview. He smiled politely and nodded his head.

"You've decided. All right, we'll set a date."

He didn't even ask why now. Seunggyun had been ready to reply that there was finally someone outside whom he wanted to see.

Perhaps this feeling he had for her was a kind of addiction; it's not as if he hadn't thought of. Yeonsun could be a new kind of monster, a monster's monster who had ruled over them, subconsciously addicting them to her so they'd help her escape back into the world.

Even so, he had a feeling that, if he could see her face again, he'd remember it this time. With just one more look, he would remember her face forever.

"Thank you for saving me, but I don't feel the same way."

"Oh, Teacher, didn't I tell you? I have a boyfriend."

"But Teacher, your voice was the best part of you, how could you have sacrificed it for me?"

"I've become a murderer myself, Teacher, because of you. Will you come visit me in prison?"

"You know we can't meet like this, by law. We have no future together."

"Why did you squeeze my hand that time, you pervert? Did you think I would forget? I hate disgusting people like you."

"Teacher, I'm a lesbian."

"Actually, I prefer younger men… If only Mr. Hamin had made it out of the centre and not you."

He could go on thinking until the world ended of ways she might reject him. But a rejection would be fine. He just wanted a chance.

O

The date for his surgery was set and a send-off party arranged. The warden made a special concession to give them each three cans of beer, even for Suhyun, who wasn't old enough to drink, which gave everyone else one more. The karaoke machine, which had finally been returned, was properly used for about an hour or two before being relegated to background music for the remainder of the evening.

"There are two kinds of monsters in this world, it seems. Those who can leave here and those who never can… You are lucky to be in the former group. I'll probably leave here feet first. Cremated and locked away like biohazard waste. Who knows what diseases my ashes would spread if they were scattered? I envy you, I do. But good for you. I hope the surgery is a success." Kyoungmo's confidences had grown with the length of his beard.

"He's right, hyoung. I'm thinking of following in your footsteps soon. Maybe when wig technology improves a little, I'll come look for you"

Seunggyun grinned and they bumped fists. To think that the most powerful political figure in Korea was an institutionalised twenty-year-old. Who could have imagined such a thing? When Seunggyun first came to the centre, he thought he and the other inmates had made the world crazy. But now that he was leaving, he realised the world had always been a strange place, the inmates were just a tiny bit stranger.

He was worried most about Suhyun. Through her improved dexterity from hair-braiding, she had made an elaborate friendship bracelet for Seunggyun that she now fastened on his wrist. He ignored her sharp claws scratching at his skin. The bracelet was still a little rough and smelled faintly of earth but Seunggyun treasured it.

"Please promise me something," she said as Seunggyun tried to keep his composure.

He said he would promise her anything.

"When you die someday, don't do anything wasteful like cremation, or any of those capsules or micro-organisms or whatnot, just get interred. In a coffin with thin panels, and maybe a shroud."

"OK. I promise."

"I get all the food I want in here, I'm just thinking of my friends out there who're starving. It makes my heart break."

Seunggyun realised Suhyun's sympathy was like that of many children her age who worried about other children in starving countries, and decided to leave it at that.

"So, hyoung," said Hamin, "what do you think will be the strangest revelation once you're back out there?"

"Well. Maybe that we'd been in Seoul this whole time? Or some other place I'm very familiar with. Not that the centre would ever reveal its secrets, I guess."

"I think I know what you mean. If this place turned out to be somewhere not so far removed from our lives… That would be strange."

Seunggyun nodded his head. Sitting in silence, he stared out into the outdoor lights, which were twice as bright since Yeonsun's escape, and the darkness between them.

O

The lights of the operation theatre made the back of his eyelids white. He could see the capillaries like roads on a map. He was thinking about Yeonsun. Of an evening some time back when she was drunk from her two beers and spinning around near the benches in the centre's front lawn. She had stolen one of Kyoungmo's cigarettes, despite the fact she never smoked, and drew pictures in the air with its white trail. Or perhaps they had been letters. She seemed like she was dancing but the whole time she moved Seunggyun was fearful the ash would drop on her; it never did. As if the centre, or the whole world loved Yeonsun so much that it had moved so the ash wouldn't drop on her. What a strange being she was. One so vague she would forever escape the grinding gears of this harsh universe.

He was going to go see Yeonsun. And when he did, she would have an unreadable expression in that unknown face of hers. The operation table was cold, and the doctor was perhaps not a doctor, but Seunggyun smiled anyway. When the doctor started his anaesthesia and told him to start counting backwards, Seunggyun left behind some words instead.

"Take my voice."

Iyagi — Chapbook Series

1. — Knockoff Viagra and Jeje

Sang Young Park translated by Anton Hur

2. — Take My Voice

Serang Chung translated by Anton Hur

3. — Towards 0%

Seo Ije translated by Rachel Min Park

4. — Kyoko and Kyoji

Han Junghyun translated by Emily Yae Won

5. — The Greatest Gamble on Earth

Kwak Jaesik translated by Hyowon Yun

6. — Walk With a Goddess

Ji-min Lee translated by Paige Aniyah Morris

7. — Like a Barbie

Park Min-jung translated by Clare Richards

8. — For That Which Cannot Be Restored

Park Wanseo translated by Soobin Kim

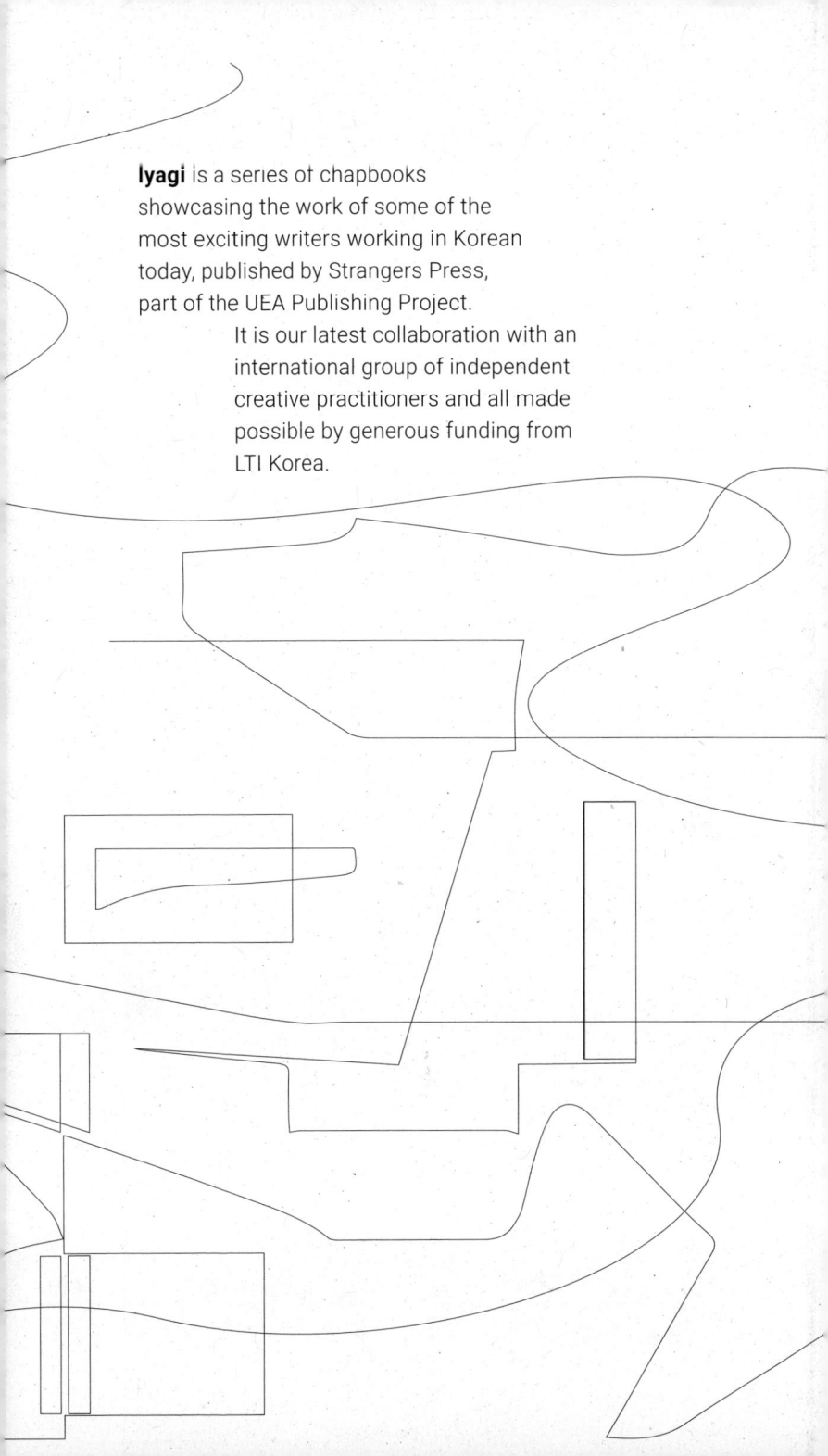

Iyagi is a series of chapbooks showcasing the work of some of the most exciting writers working in Korean today, published by Strangers Press, part of the UEA Publishing Project.

It is our latest collaboration with an international group of independent creative practitioners and all made possible by generous funding from LTI Korea.

Take My Voice
Serang Chung

Translated from Korean by
Anton Hur

First published by
Strangers Press, Norwich, 2023
part of the UEA Publishing Project

Distributed by
BookSource, UK

This book is published with the support
of the Literature Translation Institute of Korea

Printed by
Swallowtail Print, Norwich

Series editors
Nathan Hamilton & Anton Hur

Cover design and typesetting
studio aono-billson

Typefaces
Roboto / Roboto Mono
Nanum Gothic

Illustration and Design, Copyright © Nigel Aono-Billson, 2023

ISBN: 978-1-913861-52-0

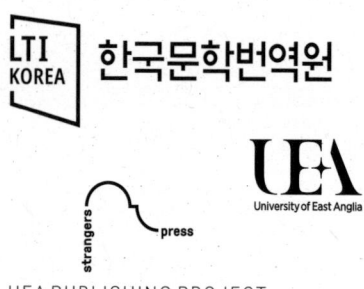

UEA PUBLISHING PROJECT
NORWICH